W9-DCB-223

*Dedicated to Mr. Robinson, my bank manager, and to the Midland Bank.*

copyright David McKee 1973
First published 1973
Library of Congress Catalog Card Number 73-2156
ISBN 0-200-72030-9 Trade

All rights reserved. No part of this publication
may be reproduced, stored in a retrieval
system, or transmitted in any form or by any
means, electronic, photocopying, recording or
otherwise, without the written permission of the
Publisher.

Weekly Reader Children's Book Club Edition

Weekly Reader Children's Book Club presents

# LORD REX

## the lion who wished

**Written and illustrated by
David McKee**

Abelard-Schuman
LONDON     NEW YORK

Lord Rex was a lion who wished.

He wished the night was not so long. He wished that he could climb trees. He wished the rain would stop falling. He always wanted things to be different from the way they were.

One day, when Lord Rex went for a walk, he met a butterfly.

"Hello!" he said. "What lovely wings you have! I wish I had Wings like that."

"You do?" asked the butterfly. "Well, since I am a magic butterfly I can grant you just one wish. You have made your wish and now you have your wings."

It was true! There, on the lion's back, were magnificent wings. Carefully Lord Rex tried them out. He really could fly! He flew up and up and up, and then he zoomed down again.

He even flew somersaults and upside down. Soon, however, he became bored with flying.

Finally he landed near an elephant who was moving a tree with his trunk. Lord Rex stared admiringly. "How strong your trunk is!" he cried. "How I wish I had a trunk like that."

"You do?" said the elephant. "Well, since I am a magic elephant, I can grant you just one wish. You have made your wish, and now you have your trunk."

Sure enough, there on the lion's face was an enormous trunk. Lord Rex thanked the elephant and went on his way. Gleefully, he swung his new trunk, using it to shift branches from his path. He used it to pick fruit, and even for scratching his back.

Just as he was becoming tired of the trunk, he saw a bird – a large bird with bright feathers. There it sat, admiring its own tail. Lord Rex looked at it enviously. "What a beautiful tail," he said. "I wish I had a tail like that."

He really wasn't surprised when the bird said, "I am a magic bird and can grant you just one wish. You have made your wish, and now you have your tail."

Slowly a magnificent tail appeared and, as he walked,
Lord Rex looked backwards so that he could gaze at it.

Because he wasn't looking where he was going, he wandered out of the jungle right into the path of a bouncing kangaroo.

"I'm sorry I knocked you over," said the kangaroo, leaping back and helping him up.

Lord Rex didn't mind. He was peering at the kangaroo's back legs. "What unusual legs," he said. "What fun to hop around! How I wish I had legs like that!"

"You do?" replied the kangaroo. "I am a magic kangaroo with the power to grant you just one wish. You have made your wish, and now you have your legs, but watch where you are going." Lord Rex jumped over a pile of stones and went off.

He bounced along until he spotted a stately giraffe. He gazed up longingly. "That neck!" he cried. "How tall it is!" He hopped over to the giraffe. "By any chance, are you a magic giraffe?" he asked eagerly. "If you are, I wish I could have a neck like yours."

"That's what I am," answered the giraffe. "You have made your wish, and now you have your neck." And, suddenly, Lord Rex and the giraffe stood face to face.

Lord Rex sniffed a flower in the grass. He poked his head between his legs, and peeked around and above the trees. Then he glanced down into a pool of water and saw a strange creature staring back at him. He laughed. "I certainly don't wish to look like you," he said. The creature laughed too—but silently. When Lord Rex stopped laughing, so did the creature.

Lord Rex bent his head to get a closer look. Then he realized he was looking at himself in the water. He looked terrible!

"Oh!" he groaned. "I've got everything I wished for—and now it's not me at all. What can I do?"

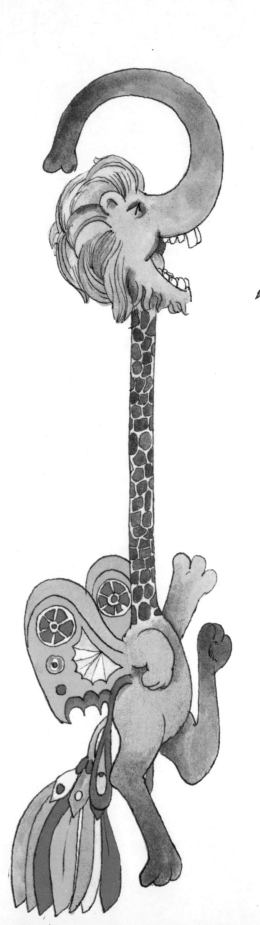

"What's wrong?" said a voice. Lord Rex turned around. There was a lion – an ordinary lion, just the way Lord Rex used to be.

"I'm what's wrong," sighed Lord Rex. "I'm ridiculous. How I wish I looked like you."

"You do? Well, since I am a magic lion . . ."

"Stop!" cried Lord Rex. "Give me one last look at myself." He gazed into the water and roared with laughter. Then he shut his eyes and said "NOW!"

When he opened his eyes again, the lion had disappeared – and so had the strange creature. Lord Rex was alone. He was himself again.

Ever since then, Lord Rex has been a happy lion. But whenever he passes a little pool, he always stops just for a moment, and takes a long, thoughtful look at the lion in the water.